ATHENA

Goddess of Wisdom, War, and Crafts

BY TERI TEMPLE

ILLUSTRATED BY ROBERT SQUIER

Published by The Child's World®
1980 Lookout Drive • Mankato, MN 56003-1705
800-599-READ • www.childsworld.com

Acknowledgments
The Child's World®: Mary Berendes, Publishing Director
The Design Lab: Design and production
Red Line Editorial: Editorial direction

Design elements: Maksym Dragunov/Dreamstime;
Dreamstime

Photographs ©: Shutterstock Images, 5; Maroš
Markovic/Shutterstock Images, 12; Shutterstock Images,
14, 18, 20; Kamira/Shutterstock Images, 22; Sergey
Rusakov/Shutterstock Images, 28

ISBN 9781614732570
LCCN 2012932433

Printed in the United States of America
Mankato, MN
December 2012
PA02157

CONTENTS

INTRODUCTION

Long ago in ancient Greece and Rome, most people believed that gods and goddesses ruled their world. Storytellers shared the adventures of these gods to help explain all the mysteries in life. The gods were immortal, meaning they lived forever. Their stories were full of love and tragedy, fearsome monsters, brave heroes, and struggles for power. The storytellers wove aspects of Greek customs and beliefs into the tales. Some stories told of the creation of the world and the origins of the gods. Others helped explain natural events such as earthquakes and storms. People believed the tales, which over time became myths.

The ancient Greeks and Romans worshiped the gods by building temples and statues in their honor. They felt the gods would protect and guide them. People passed down the myths through the generations by word of mouth. Later, famous poets such as Homer and Hesiod wrote them down. Today, these myths give us a unique look at what life was like in ancient Greece more than 2,000 years ago.

ANCIENT GREEK SOCIETIES

IN ANCIENT GREECE, CITIES, TOWNS, AND THEIR SURROUNDING FARMLANDS WERE CALLED CITY-STATES. THESE CITY-STATES EACH HAD THEIR OWN GOVERNMENTS. THEY MADE THEIR OWN LAWS. THE INDIVIDUAL CITY-STATES WERE VERY INDEPENDENT. THEY NEVER JOINED TO BECOME ONE WHOLE NATION. THEY DID, HOWEVER, SHARE A COMMON LANGUAGE, RELIGION, AND CULTURE.

CHARACTERS AND PLACES

MOUNT OLYMPUS
The mountaintop home of the 12 Olympic gods

THEBES, GREECE
A city in Greece that was built by Cadmus

ATHENS, GREECE
The capital of Greece; patron city of Athena

Aegean Sea

ANCIENT GREECE

CRETE

ANDROMEDA
(an-DRAHM-uh-duh)
Wife of the hero Perseus

ARACHNE (uh-RAK-nee)
A maiden who was turned into a spider by Athena

CADMUS (kad-MUHs)
Greek hero who built Thebes and was its first king

CASSIOPEIA
(kas-ee-oh-PEE-uh)
Mother of Andromeda; constellation in the northern sky

OLYMPIAN GODS
Demeter, Hermes, Hephaestus, Aphrodite, Ares, Hera, Zeus, Poseidon, Athena, Apollo, Artemis, and Dionysus

PARTHENON
Ancient temple of Athena in Athens, Greece

TROJAN WAR
War between the ancient Greeks and Trojans

CECROPS (SEE-krahps)
First king of Athens, Greece

GAEA (JEE-uh)
Mother Earth and one of the first elements born to Chaos; mother of the Titans, Cyclopes and Hecatoncheires

GORGONS (gawr-GUHNZ)
Three monstrous sisters with snakes for hair; can turn men to stone with their gaze

HEPHAESTUS (huh-FES-tuhs)
God of fire and metalwork; son of Zeus and Hera; married to Aphrodite

HOMER (HOH-mer)
Ancient Greek poet from the eighth century; wrote the epic poems the Iliad *and the* Odyssey

MEDUSA (muh-DOO-suh)
A snake-haired creature whose gaze can turn people to stone; mother of Pegasus; killed by Perseus

METIS (MEE-tis)
First wife of Zeus; mother of Athena

NIKE (NY-kee)
Goddess of victory; friend of Athena

ODYSSEUS (oh-DIS-ee-uhs)
Greek hero featured in the epic poems the Iliad *and the* Odyssey

PALLAS (PAL-uhs)
Childhood friend of Athena

PERSEUS (PUR-see-uhs)
Greek hero who killed Medusa; married to Andromeda

POSEIDON (puh-SY-duhn)
God of the sea and earthquakes; brother to Zeus

ZEUS (ZOOS)
Supreme ruler of the heavens and weather and of the gods who lived on Mount Olympus; youngest son of Cronus and Rhea; married to Hera; father of many gods and heroes

High atop a mountain, hidden behind the clouds was a palace of marble and gold. It was Mount Olympus, home of the Olympic gods. There were six gods in the beginning. They were the three brothers Poseidon, Hades, and Zeus. And there were the three sisters Demeter, Hestia, and Hera. They ruled over the heavens and the earth. The youngest brother, Zeus, was the king of the gods. He had fought his father for control of the universe with help from his siblings. The battle lasted ten long years. When it finally ended, peace settled over the earth. And the brothers drew lots to pick where they would rule.

To draw lots is to pick an object that represents a choice. When you pick, your decision is based on chance. Poseidon became god of the seas. Hades ruled the underworld. Zeus became god of the heavens and the earth.

Zeus wanted a queen to help him rule. He chose his cousin Metis as his first wife. She was known for her good counsel. She could offer Zeus advice that would help him be a fair and just king. Not long after their marriage, Metis discovered she was expecting their first child. Everything seemed perfect until Gaea, or Mother Earth, warned Zeus of a prophecy. A prophecy is a prediction about the future. Mother Earth told Zeus that a child born to Metis would one day overthrow him. Zeus was worried! He had done the same thing to his own father.

Zeus knew he could never let the child be born. But he did not want to lose Metis's good advice either. So he came up with a plan. He was sure it would take care of everything. Zeus challenged Metis to a shape-changing contest. He tricked her into becoming a tiny fly. Then he swallowed her up. Zeus foolishly thought all his problems were solved.

Many days later, Zeus began having horrible headaches. One day the headaches were so bad that he begged his son Hephaestus for help. Zeus asked Hephaestus to use his ax to split open his pounding head. Always a good son, Hephaestus did as he was told. Athena popped out from the split in Zeus's skull. She was fully grown and dressed in full armor. Athena introduced herself to the world with a battle cry.

Athena was a grey-eyed beauty. She became Zeus's favorite child. He gave her a strong breastplate called the Aegis. A breastplate is a piece of armor that covers the chest. The Aegis would become one of Athena's greatest weapons. Zeus even let her hold his thunderbolts. Athena was known for her wisdom and justice. These skills would help her as the goddess of war.

Athena was a young woman. But she had trouble fitting in on Mount Olympus. So she set out to find her own place in the world. Athena found a friend in Pallas. She was a daughter of the sea god Triton. Together they often practiced their fighting skills. One day during training, Athena's blow accidentally killed Pallas. Deeply sorry for the accident, Athena wanted to remember her friend always. So she set a statue of Pallas near Zeus's throne on Mount Olympus. Athena also took on her friend's name. Her followers often called her Pallas Athena.

Nike was another of Athena's constant companions. Nike was the winged goddess of victory. Athena, in a golden helmet, was often seen on the battlefield with Nike. Together they fought for just causes. With her lance and shield, Athena led armies in times of war. But in times of peace, she was able to share her skills in the arts and crafts.

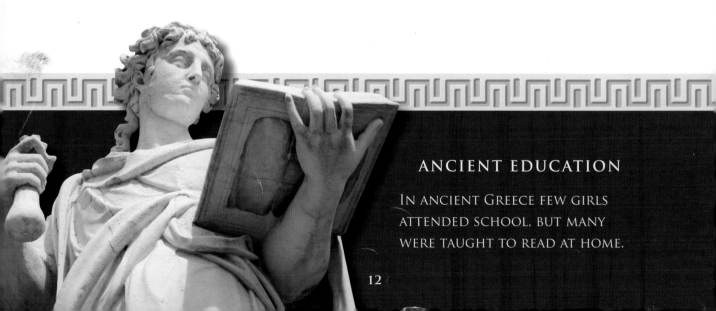

ANCIENT EDUCATION

IN ANCIENT GREECE FEW GIRLS ATTENDED SCHOOL. BUT MANY WERE TAUGHT TO READ AT HOME.

MOST CHILDREN LEARNED SOME PRACTICAL SKILLS FROM THEIR PARENTS OR
SLAVES. THE SCHOOLS TAUGHT BOYS GENERAL STUDIES, MUSIC, AND PHYSICAL
EDUCATION. OLDER BOYS ALSO RECEIVED TRAINING IN HANDLING WEAPONS.

SPIDERS

MANY SPIDERS CAN SPIN WEBS MADE OF
SILK. THIS SILK IS MADE IN THE SPIDERS'
BODIES. SPIDER WEBS CAN BE SIMPLE OR VERY
COMPLEX IN DESIGN. ONE PURPOSE IS TO

As the goddess of crafts, Athena was skilled at more than just fighting. She loved literature, poetry, music, and the arts. She also loved to invent things. She created the flute but never learned to play it very well. Athena's favorite invention was the loom for weaving. She loved to weave beautiful tapestries. A tapestry is a heavy cloth woven to show a picture.

A silly maiden named Arachne began claiming that her weaving was better than Athena's. Athena was furious. How could a simple girl compare herself to a goddess? So Athena challenged Arachne to a contest of skill. They each would be judged on one tapestry. Sitting at her loom, Athena created a perfect picture showing the splendor of the Olympian gods. Arachne's tapestry was also perfect. But Arachne's tapestry showed only how foolish the gods could be. Athena tore the tapestry to shreds in anger. She also turned Arachne into the first spider. Now Arachne would only weave spider webs.

CATCH INSECTS FOR FOOD. SPIDERS ARE NOT INSECTS, THOUGH. INSECTS HAVE SIX LEGS, BUT SPIDERS HAVE EIGHT. THEY ARE ARACHNIDS. THE ANCIENT GREEKS BELIEVED THAT THE FIRST SPIDER IN THE WORLD WAS THE MAIDEN ARACHNE. THE NAME *ARACHNE* MEANS "SPIDER" IN GREEK. FROM *ARACHNE* CAME THE WORD *ARACHNIDS*, WHICH IS ANOTHER WORD FOR SPIDERS.

Unlike other goddesses on Mount Olympus, Athena was too busy for marriage. She became the special friend to people in need. Heroes called upon her for protection. Cadmus would become one of her heroes. He was a foreign prince on a quest. Zeus had kidnapped his sister Europa. Cadmus sailed to Greece. An oracle told him that Europa was safe and well there. He was told by the oracle to end his search and stay in Greece to build a new city.

During the journey, Ares, the god of war, sent a dragon after Cadmus. The dragon attacked Cadmus and killed all of his men. Cadmus then killed the dragon. Athena told him to plant its teeth in a field. From the ground arose an army of warriors. So Athena told Cadmus to throw a stone amongst them to trick the warriors into attacking each other. The battle lasted until only five warriors were left. These five became the loyal servants of Cadmus. Together they built the city of Thebes. Cadmus became a great king and was favored by the gods. Zeus even gave Cadmus his daughter Harmonia in marriage. Thebes became one of the greatest cities in Greece.

Athena also showed favor to the handsome Perseus. He was a son of Zeus who was cast into the sea as an infant. Perseus had to fight to survive from the very start. He was sent by the king of Seriphus to collect the head of the Gorgon Medusa. This seemed an impossible task. Medusa could turn her enemies to stone with just a look. But Athena wanted Perseus to succeed.

Medusa had once been an attendant of Athena. Medusa had been very beautiful and caught the attention of Poseidon. He approached Medusa while she was visiting Athena's temple. She was enchanted by Poseidon's attention. When Athena discovered their affair, she was furious. As punishment, Athena transformed Medusa into a Gorgon. It was this creature that Perseus sought to kill.

THE GORGONS

THE GORGONS WERE THREE SISTERS. THEIR UGLINESS COULD TURN MEN TO STONE. THEY WERE THE DAUGHTERS OF THE SEA GOD PHORCYS AND THE SEA MONSTER CETO. THE GORGONS' HAIR WAS A MASS OF HISSING SNAKES. THE ANCIENT GREEKS CARVED THE GORGON'S IMAGE ONTO ARMOR TO TERRIFY THEIR ENEMIES. THEY ALSO FELT THE IMAGES PROTECTED THEM FROM EVIL SPELLS.

Perseus was sure he would succeed with Athena at his side. Together they made a plan to slay Medusa. Zeus wanted Perseus to succeed as well. So he sent his son Hermes, the god of travels, to help.

Perseus traveled to the island of the Gorgons. He brought a bronze shield of Athena and a sword of Hermes. Athena had told him what to do when he arrived. He used the shield as a mirror to look at the sisters. Perseus saw the writhing snakes they had instead of hair. He also saw the stone statues of the men who had come before him. Perseus used the reflection to find Medusa and he beheaded her. He placed Medusa's head in a bag and planned to give it to Athena. But first he had to save the life of his future bride, Andromeda.

Her mother Cassiopeia dared to compare Andromeda's beauty to that of Poseidon's sea nymphs. In anger, Poseidon sent a horrible sea monster to destroy their home. Andromeda was to be sacrificed to the monster. Her father chained Andromeda to the rocks in his kingdom of Ethiopia. On his way home Perseus saw the beautiful maiden. He immediately fell in love. Perseus killed the monster using Hermes's sword. Together they returned to give Athena Medusa's head. Athena put the head onto her shield where it helped her in battle.

ANDROMEDA AND CASSIOPEIA CONSTELLATIONS

ANDROMEDA AND CASSIOPEIA ARE CONSTELLATIONS IN THE NORTHERN SKY.

The five brightest stars of the Cassiopeia constellation form a large *W* shape. The ancient Greeks believed Poseidon placed Cassiopeia in the sky as a punishment for her pride. In art, she is usually shown sitting on a throne combing her hair.

Athena found someone similar to herself in Odysseus. He was the Greek king of Ithaca. They shared many of the same qualities. Like Athena, Odysseus was smart, just, and clever. He enjoyed Athena's protection during the Trojan War, but he really needed protection on his journey home.

The other gods wanted to punish Odysseus for defeating the Trojans. They had supported the Trojans during the war. So the gods created many problems for Odysseus as he sailed back to his wife and son. Odysseus was a prisoner of the sea nymph Calypso for seven years. After finally escaping, he sailed through storms and shipwrecks. Odysseus had angered the sea god Poseidon when he blinded his son Polyphemus. Athena did not want to anger the other gods. So she could only offer Odysseus guidance and advice in his dreams.

HOMER

HOMER WAS A GREEK POET WHO LIVED IN THE EIGHTH CENTURY BC. HE WAS THOUGHT TO BE BLIND. HOMER IS BEST KNOWN FOR HIS EPIC POEMS THE *ILIAD* AND THE *ODYSSEY*. THEY TELL THE TALE OF ODYSSEUS, AN ANCIENT GREEK SAILOR. THE POEMS COVER HIS ADVENTURES AS HE SAILED OFF TO FIGHT THE TROJAN WAR. MUCH OF WHAT WE KNOW ABOUT GREEK MYTHOLOGY COMES FROM HOMER AND HIS POEMS.

After ten long years Odysseus finally returned to his home in Ithaca. Athena warned him that many men wished to marry his wife. Since Odysseus had been gone so long, they were sure he was dead. Athena helped disguise Odysseus. He then defeated more than 100 rivals. He regained his throne and his wife.

While the heroes celebrated Athena, her uncle Poseidon was often at odds with her. He was not a very clever god and was often frustrated by Athena. As the god of the sea, he wanted the waters for his creatures alone. Poseidon was furious when Athena taught men how to build ships. After that, humans sailed all over his oceans and seas. After Poseidon created the horse, Athena created the bridle and chariot. The chariot was a two-wheeled horse-drawn carriage. A bridle is made of straps and is used to control a horse. The bridle and chariot were used for hunting or racing. They also served the humans well in wars. Again Athena was shown to be more clever than Poseidon.

Then the day came when they each claimed the city-state of Athens. Athena and Poseidon both wished to become its patron. A patron is a protector of a place. Cecrops was the first king of Athens. He was half-human and half-snake. He came up with a contest to determine who it would be. Cecrops asked Athena and Poseidon to each offer a gift to the city of Athens. The winner would be the one whose gift was deemed most valuable. Poseidon was ready for the challenge.

Poseidon chose to go first. He wanted to prove his worth. He took his trident and struck the earth with it. A trident is a spear with three points. Poseidon was so powerful that the water burst forth from the ground and formed a well. The people of the city were amazed. Their amazement did not last long, though. As the god of the sea, the water Poseidon had brought forth was salty. Cecrops did not think that would be too helpful to his city's people. Poor Poseidon was beside himself. Next up was Athena.

Athena used her spear to create a hole in the ground. She kneeled and planted an olive branch in the space. An olive tree grew from the branch. The ancient Greeks could harvest the olives for food. The people were very impressed with Athena's gift. Cecrops decided that Athena's gift was indeed more useful. He declared Athena the winner and the patron goddess of his city. The city was named Athens after Athena. In his anger, Poseidon caused the whole area to flood. Eventually though, Athena and Poseidon would work together for the sake of the people.

Nearly everyone loved and worshiped Athena. As the goddess of war she was often sought out for her sound judgment and good counsel. She was also a fierce warrior. She was sure to gain victory in battle with Nike at her side. Temples and shrines were built all over Greece in her honor. Festivals were held during the summer. The ancient Greeks gathered to pay tribute to Athena with competitions in athletics and music.

The most famous temple to Athena was the Parthenon. The Parthenon was an ancient temple in Athens, Greece. It was built between 447 BC and 432 BC. It sat on a hill known as the Acropolis above the city. The ancient Greeks dedicated the temple to Athena because she was the patron goddess of their city. The temple once held a great statue of the goddess covered in gold and ivory. Although her temple now stands in ruins, Athena remains an important part of the history of ancient Greece. Her stories will continue to be told for years to come.

MINERVA

MINERVA WAS ONE OF ANCIENT ROME'S MOST IMPORTANT GODDESSES. ROME CONQUERED GREECE IN THE THIRD TO SECOND CENTURY BC. THE ROMANS ADOPTED MANY ASPECTS OF GREEK CULTURE. THEY ESPECIALLY LIKED THE GREEKS' STORIES ABOUT THE GODS. ATHENA BECAME THEIR GODDESS MINERVA.

PRINCIPAL GODS OF GREEK MYTHOLOGY –
A FAMILY TREE

EROS

ARES **HEBE** **HEPHAESTUS** **ATHENA** **PERSEPHONE** **APOLLO** **ARTEMIS** **HERMES** **APHRODITE**

ZEUS **MAIA** **ZEUS** **DIONE**

POSEIDON **HADES** **HESTIA** **HERA** **ZEUS** **DEMETER** **ATLAS** **PROMETHEUS** **EPIMETHEUS**

IAPETUS

LETO **ZEUS**

CRONUS **RHEA** **COEUS** **PHOEBE** **OCEANUS** **TETHYS**

GAEA
(Earth)

URANUS
(Heaven)

THE ROMAN GODS

A s the Roman Empire expanded by conquering new lands the Romans often took on aspects of the customs and beliefs of the people they conquered. From the ancient Greeks they took their arts and sciences. They also adopted many of their gods and the myths that went with them into their religious beliefs. While the names were changed, the stories and legends found a new home.

Zeus: *Jupiter*
King of the Gods, God of Sky and Storms
Symbols: *Eagle and Thunderbolt*

Hera: *Juno*
Queen of the Gods, Goddess of Marriage
Symbols: *Peacock, Cow, and Crow*

Poseidon: *Neptune*
God of the Sea and Earthquakes
Symbols: *Trident, Horse, and Dolphin*

Hades: *Pluto*
God of the Underworld
Symbols: *Helmet, Metals, and Jewels*

Athena: *Minerva*
Goddess of Wisdom, War, and Crafts
Symbols: *Owl, Shield, and Olive Branch*

Ares: *Mars*
God of War
Symbols: *Vulture and Dog*

Artemis: *Diana*
Goddess of Hunting and Protector of Animals
Symbols: *Stag and Moon*

Apollo: *Apollo*
God of the Sun, Healing, Music, and Poetry
Symbols: *Laurel, Lyre, Bow, and Raven*

Hephaestus: *Vulcan*
God of Fire, Metalwork, and Building
Symbols: *Fire, Hammer, and Donkey*

Aphrodite: *Venus*
Goddess of Love and Beauty
Symbols: *Dove, Sparrow, Swan, and Myrtle*

Eros: *Cupid*
God of Love
Symbols: *Quiver and Arrows*

Hermes: *Mercury*
God of Travels and Trade
Symbols: *Staff, Winged Sandals, and Helmet*

FURTHER INFORMATION

BOOKS

Green, Jen. *Ancient Greek Myths*. New York: Gareth Stevens, 2010.

O'Connor, George. *Athena: Grey-Eyed Goddess*. New York: First Second, 2010.

Stowell, Louie, ed. *Odyssey*. London: Usborne, 2011.

WEB SITES

Visit our Web site for links about Athena: **childsworld.com/links**

Note to Parents, Teachers, and Librarians: We routinely verify our Web links to make sure they are safe and active sites. So encourage your readers to check them out!

INDEX